For Liza Baker Stock,
who knew and loved Martha first.
—S.B.

For Ben and Ellyn, fab kids
who never have to say sorry … often!
—B.W.

Little, Brown Books for Young Readers

Hachette Book Group • 237 Park Avenue, New York, NY 10017
Visit our Web site at www.lb-kids.com

Little, Brown Books for Young Readers is a division of Hachette Book Group, Inc.
The Little, Brown name and logo are trademarks of Hachette Book Group, Inc.

First Edition: May 2009

Library of Congress Cataloging-in-Publication Data

Berger, Samantha.
  Martha doesn't say sorry / by Samantha Berger ; illustrated by Bruce Whatley.—1st ed.
    p. cm.
  Summary: Young Martha learns that she must apologize for her bad behavior if she wants people to cooperate with her.
  ISBN 978-0-316-06682-2
  [1. Behavior—Fiction. 2. Apologizing—Fiction.] I. Whatley, Bruce, ill. II. Title. III. Title: Martha doesn't say sorry.
  PZ7.B452136Mar 2009
  [E]—dc22
                                        2008016769

10 9 8 7 6 5 4 3 2   Printed in Singapore

The illustrations for this book were done in watercolor and colored pencil.
The text was set in Barbera, and the display type is Carl Beck.

Martha
doesn't say sorry!

by Samantha Berger   ⌇   illustrated by Bruce Whatley

LITTLE, BROWN AND COMPANY
Books for Young Readers
New York   Boston

There are many things Martha does,
but apologizing isn't one of them.

She does give hugs.

She does share her snack.

She does make presents.

She does read stories.

But Martha doesn't say sorry.

Sometimes Martha does things
that are...not so nice.
She sticks her tongue out.

She throws things.

She kicks pretty hard, too.

But Martha doesn't say sorry.

One day Martha does something not
so nice to her mother...

and her father...

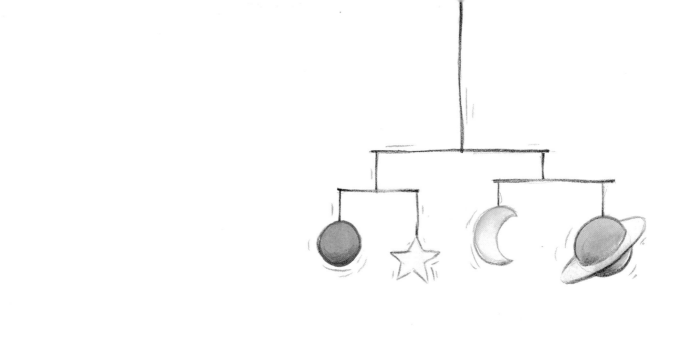

and her baby brother.

Martha is really having a day.
She gets a Time-Out to think.
She knows where it all went wrong.
She wants to make it right...

But Martha doesn't say sorry.

Martha does, however,
want a cookie!

But Martha's mother doesn't give cookies to people who don't say sorry.

Martha does, however,
want a piggyback ride.

But Martha's father doesn't give piggyback rides to people who don't say sorry.

Martha does, however,
want a hug.

But Martha's baby brother
doesn't give hugs to people
who don't say sorry.

Fine!

Martha does not have a cookie,
a piggyback ride, or a hug.
Who needs them, anyway?

Martha thinks it over.

She thinks and thinks and thinks it over.

Then she says something very, very softly.

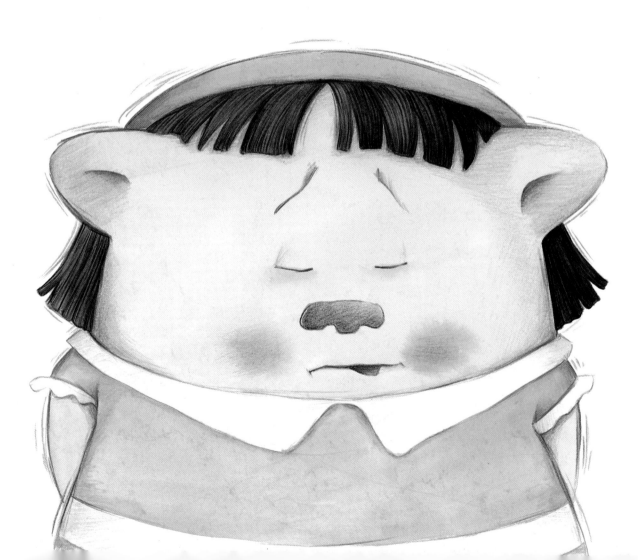

I'm Sorry.

But nobody hears her.

She says it again, just a tiny bit louder.
But only a tiny bit...

I'm Sorry.

And still no one hears her.
So she says it again, a little bit louder.

I'm Sorry.

"What?" asks her mother.
"What?" asks her father.
"Fwa?" asks her baby brother.

I'm Sorry!

Martha's family is glad Martha says sorry.
Deep down, Martha is glad, too.

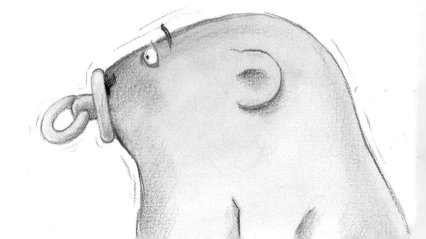

Now, every once in a while
when Martha does something not so nice...

Martha apologizes...

I'm Sorry!

as nicely as she possibly can.